First Hardcover Edition, July 2021
1 3 5 7 9 10 8 6 4 2

ISBN 978-1-368-06457-6
FAC-034274-21141
Library of Congress Control Number: 2020943705
Printed in the United States of America

Visit www.disneybooks.com

Disney

Tim Burton's
THE NIGHTMARE BEFORE CHRISTMAS
13 Days of Christmas

Written by **Steven Davison** and **Carolyn Gardner**
Illustrated by **Jerrod Maruyama**
Designed by **David Roe**

Disney PRESS
Los Angeles • New York

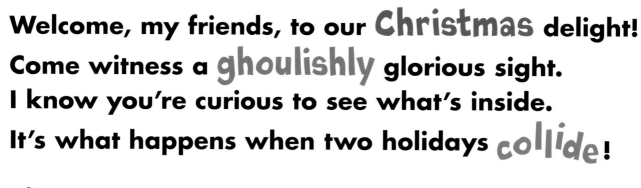

Welcome, my friends, to our **Christmas** delight!
Come witness a **ghoulishly** glorious sight.
I know you're curious to see what's inside.
It's what happens when two holidays collide!

**On the first day of Christmas,
my ghoul love gave to me
a star for my
fortune-card tree.**

On the second day of Christmas,
my ghoul love gave to me
two true-love potions
and a star for my fortune-card tree.

On the third day of Christmas,
my ghoul love gave to me
three life lines extending,
two true-love potions,
and a star for my fortune-card tree.

On the fourth day of Christmas,
my ghoul love gave to me
four wheels of fortune,
three life lines extending,
two true-love potions,
and a star for my fortune-card tree.

On the fifth day of Christmas,
my ghoul love gave to me

five lucky charms,

four wheels of fortune,
three life lines extending,
two true-love potions,
and a star for my fortune-card tree.

On the sixth day of Christmas,
my ghoul love gave to me
six mystic mirrors,
five lucky charms,
four wheels of fortune,
three life lines extending,
two true-love potions,
and a star for my fortune-card tree.

On the seventh day of Christmas,
my ghoul love gave to me
seven pearls of wisdom,
six mystic mirrors,
five lucky charms,
four wheels of fortune,
three life lines extending,
two true-love potions,
and a star for my fortune-card tree.

On the eighth day of Christmas,
my ghoul love gave to me
eight orbs of knowledge,
seven pearls of wisdom,
six mystic mirrors,
five lucky charms,
four wheels of fortune,
three life lines extending,
two true-love potions,
and a star for my fortune-card tree.

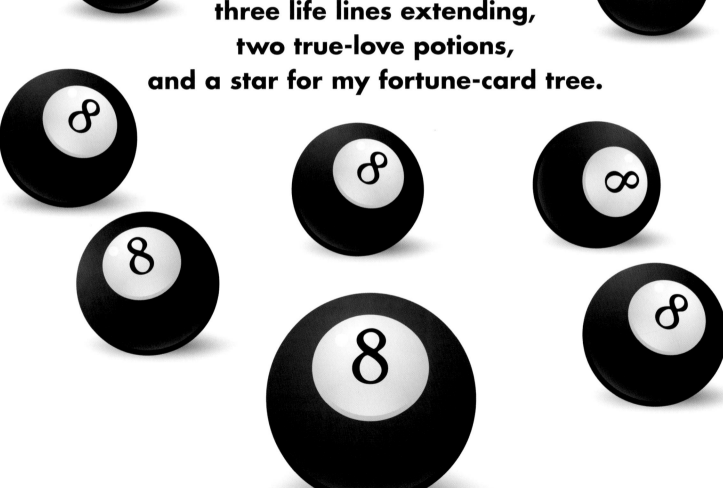

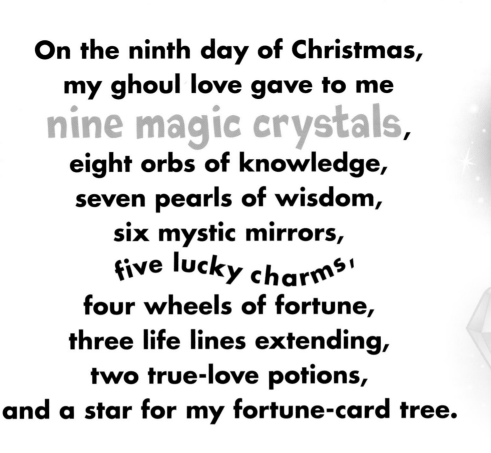

On the ninth day of Christmas,
my ghoul love gave to me
nine magic crystals,
eight orbs of knowledge,
seven pearls of wisdom,
six mystic mirrors,
five lucky charms,
four wheels of fortune,
three life lines extending,
two true-love potions,
and a star for my fortune-card tree.

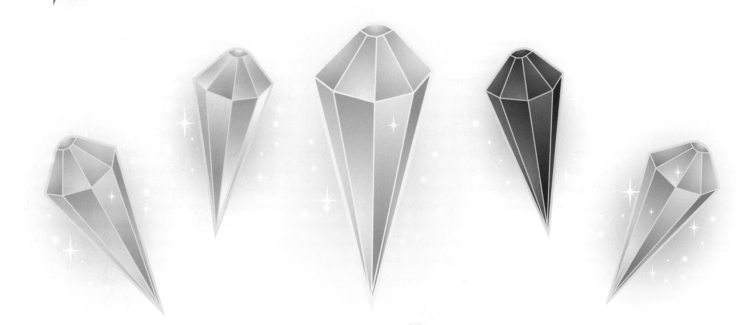

On the tenth day of Christmas,
my ghoul love gave to me
ten telling tea leaves,
nine magic crystals,
eight orbs of knowledge,
seven pearls of wisdom,
six mystic mirrors,
five lucky charms,
four wheels of fortune,
three life lines extending,
two true-love potions,
and a star for my fortune-card tree.

On the eleventh day of Christmas,
my ghoul love gave to me
eleven candles floating,
ten telling tea leaves,
nine magic crystals,
eight orbs of knowledge,
seven pearls of wisdom,
six mystic mirrors,
five lucky charms,
four wheels of fortune,
three life lines extending,
two true-love potions,
and a star for my fortune-card tree.

On the twelfth day of Christmas,
my ghoul love gave to me
twelve twinkling star signs,
eleven candles floating,
ten telling tea leaves,
nine magic crystals,
eight orbs of knowledge,
seven pearls of wisdom,
six mystic mirrors,
five lucky charms,
four wheels of fortune,
three life lines extending,
two true-love potions,
and a star for my fortune-card tree.

On the thirteenth day of Christmas,
my ghoul love gave to me
thirteen rings of power,
twelve twinkling star signs,
eleven candles floating,
ten telling tea leaves,
nine magic crystals,
eight orbs of knowledge,
seven pearls of wisdom,
six mystic mirrors,
five lucky charms,
four wheels of fortune,
three life lines extending,
two true-love potions . . .

. . . and a star for my
fortune-card tree.

Scary Christmas!